The TWINS AND THE BIRD OF DARKNESS

A HERO TALE FROM THE CARIBBEAN

BY Robert D. San Souci

ILLUSTRATED BY Terry Widener

SIMON & SCHUSTER BOOKS FOR YOUNG READERS

New York · London · Toronto · Sydney · Singapore

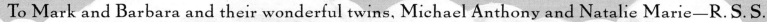

To Mark and Barbara and their wonderful twins, Michael Anthony and Natalie Marie—R. S. S.

For my mom—T. W.

SIMON & SCHUSTER BOOKS FOR YOUNG READERS
An imprint of Simon & Schuster Children's Publishing Division
1230 Avenue of the Americas, New York, New York 10020

Text copyright © 2002 by Robert D. San Souci
Illustrations copyright © 2002 by Terry Widener

Book design by Paula Winicur
The text for this book is set in Pabst.
The illustrations are rendered in Gulden acrylics on Strathmore paper.
Printed in Hong Kong

2 4 6 8 10 9 7 5 3 1

Library of Congress Cataloging-in-Publication Data
San Souci, Robert D. Twins and the Bird of Darkness : a hero tale from the Caribbean /
by Robert D. San Souci ; illustrated by Terry Widener.—1st ed.
p. cm.
Summary : When the Bird of Darkness takes Princess Marie, twin brothers Soliday, who is brave and kind,
and Salacota, who is cowardly, set off to fight the beast and rescue the princess.

ISBN 0-689-83343-1

[1. Folklore—Caribbean area.] I. Widener, Terry, ill. II. Title.
PZ8.1.S227 Tw 2002 398.2`09729`02—dc21 [E] 99-058950

first
edition

ONCE THERE WAS A KING who ruled a pretty island in the Caribbean. He was greater than the fabled Asante kings of Africa, who were his own ancestors. But he was a good man as well as a powerful monarch, so he governed wisely and justly. In return, heaven gave him a graceful, loving, intelligent daughter, Marie, whose fame spread to the ends of the earth. The kingdom prospered until it became the fairest of the flowered islands called the Antilles.

Life was wonderful, until the monstrous Bird of Darkness came from behind the horizon to trouble the island. The creature had seven heads, each covered with shining feathers of a different color: red, orange, yellow, green, blue, violet, and purple. It had immense claws of gold and seven cruel golden beaks.

Most terrible were its vast wings, which were blacker than the heart of night. They swallowed the sunshine and moonlight and starlight. When the bird perched on the island's highest peak and unfolded its wings, they swirled and spread across the sky like ink clouds in a pool of water. Noon turned to midnight.

As the frightened people huddled in torchlight and candlelight, the king sent his bravest soldier to climb the mountain to ask the Bird of Darkness why it had come.

When he stood before the creature, the man called out,

"Greetings, great Bird of Darkness.
Greetings, bringer of endless night.
Why have you come to trouble our island?
What do you seek so far from home?"

Then the bird sang in seven voices that blended as one,

"Greetings to you, courageous soldier.
Greetings to you, brave messenger.
I claim the king's daughter as my tribute,
Or I will never leave this place."

When the soldier reported this, the island's ruler refused to surrender his daughter. He sent his army to drive the bird away, but the monster easily defeated the king's forces.

Darkness lay thick and chill over forest and meadow. Crops withered and children wept and fearful creatures of the night made the land their own.

Princess Marie, who loved her people and ached to see their unhappiness, resolved to end their misery. The courageous young woman left her father's palace secretly and journeyed to the mountaintop where the Bird of Darkness brooded. She was filled with dread of the monster, and sadness because she might never see her father again. But she bravely gave herself up to the creature. With a bellow of triumph it snatched her in its claws, rose into the air, and carried her to its home beyond the horizon.

Though the darkness was lifted from his island, a gloom settled over the king. He had his drums beaten throughout the land, promising that the man who found and slew the seven-headed beast and returned his daughter to him would be rewarded threefold. He would be given Marie's hand in marriage, half the kingdom to rule, and half the king's fortune.

Many men bravely sailed beyond the horizon in search of the Bird of Darkness. None returned.

Now it happened there were twin brothers, Soliday and Salacota, who were so alike in appearance and voice that even their old grandmother, who raised them, had difficulty telling them apart. But Soliday was good-hearted and brave, while Salacota was mean-spirited and cowardly. Yet Soliday loved his brother and hoped that Salacota would someday have a change of heart.

They were so poor that, as children, the boys had only banana leaves to wear. They lived in a hut by the sea, and Soliday gathered shellfish to eat and to trade for cooking oil or meat. Sometimes, when he went to market, he found colorful scraps of cloth. When he had enough, he asked his grandmother to sew him a coat of forty colors to wear over his rags.

Salacota did no work. He complained because he had no fine clothes and not enough to eat. He was jealous of his brother's colorful coat, but he was unwilling to hunt for scraps himself. So he went about looking patched and ragged.

When Soliday heard the king's drumming, he said, "I will go and slay the Bird of Darkness and rescue Marie, the king's daughter." He had often seen her from a distance as she went on her daily visits outside the palace walls. He watched with admiration as she gave help to those in need. He had been too shy to approach her, but he remained enchanted by her lovely face that seemed to him the perfect reflection of her generous, loving heart.

"You're a fool, brother, even to think such a thing," Salacota mocked him. "How will you reach the Bird of Darkness without a boat? How will you kill the beast without weapons?"

But Soliday said to their grandmother, "Once again I need your help. Surely you know how I can go and slay the Bird of Darkness and save the princess Marie."

At first the old woman tried to discourage him. But when she saw that his mind was made up, she gave him her last few coins, saying, "Use these to pay the *quimboiseur*, the sorcerer, who lives in the forest. He will tell you how to find and kill the Bird of Darkness."

Soliday asked his brother to come with him, since the sorcerer's hut was far away and the forest was filled with fierce beasts. But Salacota said, "The woods are dangerous, and wizards are worse. You'd do better spending Grandmother's money on food and clothes for us both."

So Soliday braved the wilds alone and found the *quimboiseur*'s hut. In return for half the coins, the wizard prepared him a magic ointment. "Smear this on an arrow and shoot the monster," the wizard said. "But the arrow must be fletched with seven of the bird's feathers, each a different color."

Then the sorcerer gave him seven beads—one for every color of the beast's heads—saying, "Each day trade one of these for a feather. When you have seven feathers, fashion your arrow. On the eighth day slay the beast." Then the man told Soliday how to find the island beyond the horizon, where the bird dwelt.

So Soliday took the beads and the ointment and returned home. There he used the remaining coins to purchase a small boat.

When Salacota saw the beads and the ointment, he decided that Soliday was not such a fool after all. As he watched his brother prepare his boat for the sea-crossing, he thought greedily of the bride and riches Soliday might win. So Salacota said, "Brother, I can't let you make such a risky voyage alone. I have decided to go with you. Any dangers we will face together."

"And any rewards we will share equally," said good-hearted Soliday. Then he added, "The only thing that matters to me is freeing Princess Marie from danger. To know that she is safe— this is all the reward I desire."

Their grandmother waved from shore as the young men set sail. Soliday stood bravely in the bow in his forty-colored coat; Salacota huddled miserably in the stern.

As their island home dwindled behind them, the vast silence of the sea gathered around them. To Soliday, it held the promise of rescuing Marie and restoring her to her father; but, to Salacota, it was a source of chills, seasickness, and fear—evils he could endure only because of promised riches and rewards. Soliday was grateful to have his brother as his companion, but Salacota thought only of his own discomfort.

Soon they reached the Great Open, the measureless sea beyond the sight of land. Suddenly a long black fin cut the water beside them. Salacota began to sob with terror. But Soliday put his finger to his lips to hush Salacota. Then he hugged his brother to give him courage. The shark circled the boat several times, then dove and did not reappear.

On they sailed, caught in the current, rising and falling on the ocean swells.

"We are riding the horizon!" cried Soliday excitedly.

But Salacota was so uneasy, he shifted from side to side of the boat like a trapped animal. Finally Soliday had to warn him, "Sit still, brother! You're going to capsize us!"

Twilight turned into night as black as the shadows beneath the wings of the Bird of Darkness. The brothers shared a blanket. All night Soliday kept watch while his brother slept.

When morning pearled the ocean, Soliday shook his brother awake, crying, "Look! There is the island the sorcerer spoke of!"

Ahead, misty blue peaks rose from a nest of green forest. Circling gulls called cheerfully. The rising breeze swept them shoreward.

Salacota complained that he was hungry and thirsty. Soliday let him take a bigger share of their food and water.

When they landed, Salacota said he was too weary to search for the Bird of Darkness. With a sigh Soliday, taking a single red bead, set out through the forest toward the mountains, where he felt certain he would find the creature. He left his bow, arrows, and the other beads in Salacota's keeping.

Beyond the trees he found a narrow trail that zigzagged up the mountain. Far behind, Salacota watched his brother in his colorful coat until a bend in the path hid him from view.

After a long, hard climb Soliday came to a gigantic tree. At its base, in a cage of twisted roots, was the princess Marie. Scattered everywhere were the bones of others who had tried to rescue her.

On the topmost branch of the tree sat the Bird of Darkness. It seemed to doze, with its night-wings wrapped around its body; but at Soliday's approach, it stirred and unfolded them. Then its heads blazed rainbow-bright against their fluttering darkness.

Soliday stood at the foot of the tree and called,

"Good morning to you, Bird of
    Darkness!
Good morning to you, noble creature!
I am Soliday who greets you.
I have come to strike a bargain."

The bird responded,

"Good morning, Soliday, so far from
    home,
I'll strike the bargain I struck with
    others:
You give me your eyes and liver,
I'll give you swift death in return."

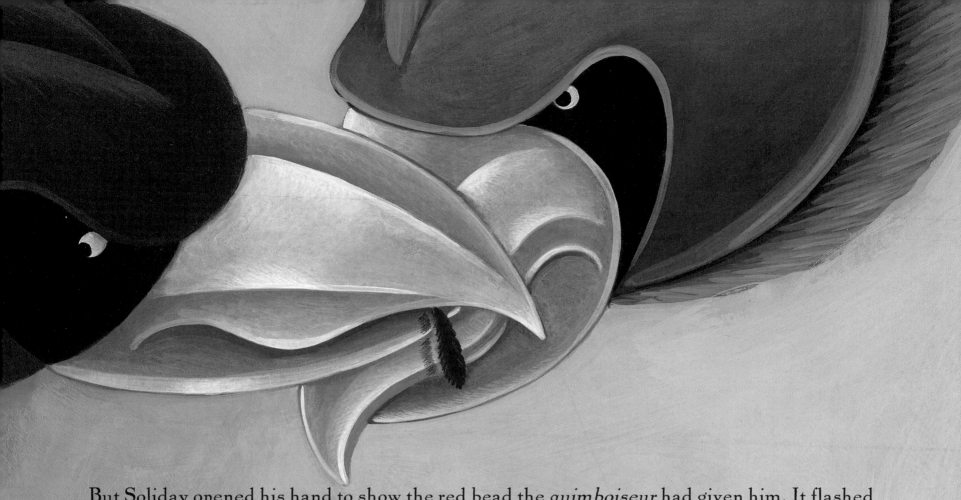

But Soliday opened his hand to show the red bead the *quimboiseur* had given him. It flashed like the rarest of jewels, the purest of rubies. The Bird of Darkness gazed eagerly at the bead.

Then Soliday sang,

"All I ask is one red feather,
In return for this rare treasure.
Strike this bargain, spare one feather,
Tomorrow I'll bring a rarer treasure."

Eagerly the bird plucked a red plume from its neck and dropped it down to Soliday. In return, the young man tossed the bead high. The bird caught it in one of its gold beaks and set it in a hollow of the tree.

Then Soliday left, pausing to whisper words of hope to the imprisoned princess.

Each morning for seven days Soliday returned to the Bird of Darkness, carrying a different-colored bead. Each day the creature surrendered one feather in payment.

On the evening of the seventh day Soliday sat on the beach, fletching his arrow with the seven feathers, creating an arrow as glorious as a rainbow. He begged his brother to accompany him the next morning, but Salacota was afraid to face the Bird of Darkness.

At dawn on the eighth day Soliday smeared the arrow tip with the sorcerer's ointment. Once again Soliday asked his brother to accompany him. And once again Salacota refused.

As before, the bird greeted Soliday in the hope that he had brought another treasure. But this time, Soliday shouted,

"Good morning to you, Bird of Darkness!
Good morning to you, wretched creature!
This is Soliday who warns you.
You must die on this bright morning!"

At this the bird flew down, its claws outstretched to rip Soliday limb from limb.

Quickly Soliday drew his bow from under his forty-colored coat and let his magic arrow fly. It buried itself in the heart of the seven-headed beast, which gave a screech that rebounded from horizon to horizon, so that Soliday had to press his hands to his ears to keep his head from bursting. It crumpled to earth, its massive wings catching on the tree branches, which held it a moment, before the weight of its huge body dragged it to the ground with the sound of expanses of silk tearing top to bottom.

Then Soliday tried to release Princess Marie, but the roots imprisoning her were too thick and tough. He would have to return to the boat, where there was an ax he could use to free her. Before he left, she handed her ring to him through the branches, saying, "Keep this as a sign that you have saved me and won my heart."

Soliday took the gold beaks from the seven-headed beast to prove he had slain the creature. With these wrapped in his coat he raced back down the mountain path.

Meanwhile Salacota's curiosity about how matters were going overcame his fear. He climbed rapidly up the path, even as Soliday hurried down. At a curve the two collided and Soliday tumbled into a ravine.

When Salacota looked down, Soliday cried, "Help me, brother! I must get my ax to free Princess Marie."

Seeing his chance to claim the princess and the reward, Salacota left his twin where he had fallen. He fetched the ax and hurried to release the princess, pretending to be Soliday.

When Marie asked about his colorful coat, the ring she had given him, and the golden beaks, he said, "I lost them in my eagerness to rescue you." Because Salacota's face and voice were so like his brother's, Marie did not realize the trick he played.

Salacota took the seven heads of the bird—though Soliday still had the golden beaks—as false proof of his courage. With Marie he sailed home, where the king welcomed them with great rejoicing. He sent his drummers throughout the land to announce that Marie would marry the man who had rescued her.

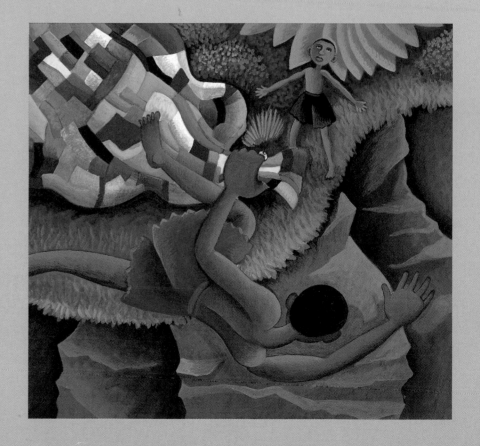

But sharp-witted Marie was troubled by changes she saw in her husband-to-be. He had been brave and kind and loving in the shadow of the deadly Bird of Darkness, but in her father's safe palace, he seemed the opposite. She asked her father to put off their marriage for a year and a day, for she was uneasy about her husband-to-be. She hoped that time would restore what seemed lacking in his soul—and would return the love that had gone out of her heart. The king agreed, so Salacota had to wait to claim the woman and the fortune that rightfully belonged to Soliday.

While Salacota waited, he grew fat and lazy and indulged himself in rich foods. He had fine clothes made; he even had special sandals fashioned that were decorated with golden images of the Bird of Darkness. Wherever he went, he wanted people to recognize and honor him as the one who had slain the monster.

Back on the island beyond the horizon, Soliday refused to give up hope. He used the golden beaks—each as hard as a diamond—to cut handholds and footholds in the ravine wall. He drank water from a mountain stream and ate berries and roots and bark.

In time he climbed free. At the shore he made a raft of logs tied with vines. Using a branch as a paddle, he pushed out to sea. His coat, tied between two poles, served as a sail.

His progress was slow. The sun burned him by day and the fog chilled him at night. Sharks circled his raft. His food and water gave out. He could only moisten his head and rinse his mouth with seawater. Again and again he kissed the ring Marie had given him, clinging to hope.

At last, one evening a year after he left, he saw the dark shape of his home island floating on the horizon.

Soliday began to paddle furiously, making landfall at dawn. He ran to the king's palace and knocked at the gate.

"What do you want?" asked the Captain of the Guard.

"I killed the Bird of Darkness," answered Soliday. "I have come to claim the hand of Princess Marie."

"Impossible," said the Captain of the Guard. "The hero Soliday killed the Bird of Darkness. He brought the creature's seven heads as proof. Tomorrow he marries the king's daughter. Whatever's afoot, you had better go away."

But Soliday unwrapped the seven golden beaks he had bundled in his coat. "I took these from the Bird of Darkness. If my twin presented the heads, they had no beaks, because I had already claimed them when I first slew the monster."

The captain shook his head, saying, "Surely what you say is true." Then he went to tell the king what he had seen.

The king hurried out, followed by Marie. The ruler gasped in wonder at the seven golden beaks. But Marie cried out joyfully when she saw Soliday in his colorful coat, proudly displaying the ring she had given him.

Soldiers were sent to find Salacota, who was attempting to escape disguised as a servant. Soliday recognized his brother, but would not betray him. But Marie spotted the golden sandals, which Salacota had refused to leave behind. So he was caught.

The king would have executed him on the spot, but Soliday pleaded for his brother's life. Though doubtful, the king granted his request.

At this, Salacota burst into tears of heartfelt remorse and vowed, "I will be your truest friend, Soliday. I will be the brother I have failed to be for all these years."

So Soliday married the princess and brought his grandmother to live in the king's palace. So many rewards had come to him for slaying the Bird of Darkness: Salacota's unfailing loyalty was one of the most satisfying.

But the greatest reward was the love of Princess Marie; often Soliday would squeeze her hand as they walked side by side, as if to assure himself she was no dream, and her loving kiss in return filled him with joy beyond all bounds.

AUTHOR'S NOTE

This tale is composited in the main
from thirteen variant tales gathered on
the Caribbean Island of Guadeloupe
and published in Elsie Clews Parsons's
*Folk-Lore of the Antilles, French and
English* (*Memoirs of the American
Folk-Lore Society*, Volume XXVI, 1943),
grouped under the headings "Twin
Brothers: Seven Tongues" and "The
Beast That Keeps the Country Dark";
several tales in Philip Sherlock's *West
Indian Folk-tales*; and Lafcaido Hearn's
narrative, "Ti Canotie," a chapter in his
Two Years in the French West Indies.
This story pattern has its roots in stories
originally brought from Europe, such as
"The Three Princesses in Whiteland," by
the Brothers Grimm.

GLOSSARY

Antilles* (On-teeyl): the islands of
the West Indies; *Mer des Antilles**
(Mehr-de-zon-teeyl) is the
Caribbean Sea

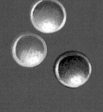

Asante* (Uh-SAN-tay): a people living in
Ghana, on the West Coast of Africa

Quimboiseur* (kwim-bwah-sur):
a wizard

*Note: French stresses all syllables
equally; the African usage stresses the
middle syllable of Asante.